THE SECRET SLIDE

A GARDEN'S GATE BOOK: THE GARDEN OF DREAMS

WRITTEN BY THOMAS MOORE   ILLUSTRATED BY REBECCA MOORE

Grosvenor House
Publishing Limited

This book is published by
Grosvenor House Publishing Ltd
Link House
140 The Broadway, Tolworth, Surrey, KT6 7HT.
www.grosvenorhousepublishing.co.uk

This book is a work of fiction. Any resemblance to
people or events, past or present, is purely coincidental.

A CIP record for this book
is available from the British Library

Paperback ISBN 978-1-80381-033-1
Hardback ISBN 978-1-80381-034-8

For Noah, Max, Tabby and Ellie.
Without you this would not have been possible.

"Go then, there are other worlds than these." - Jake Chambers.

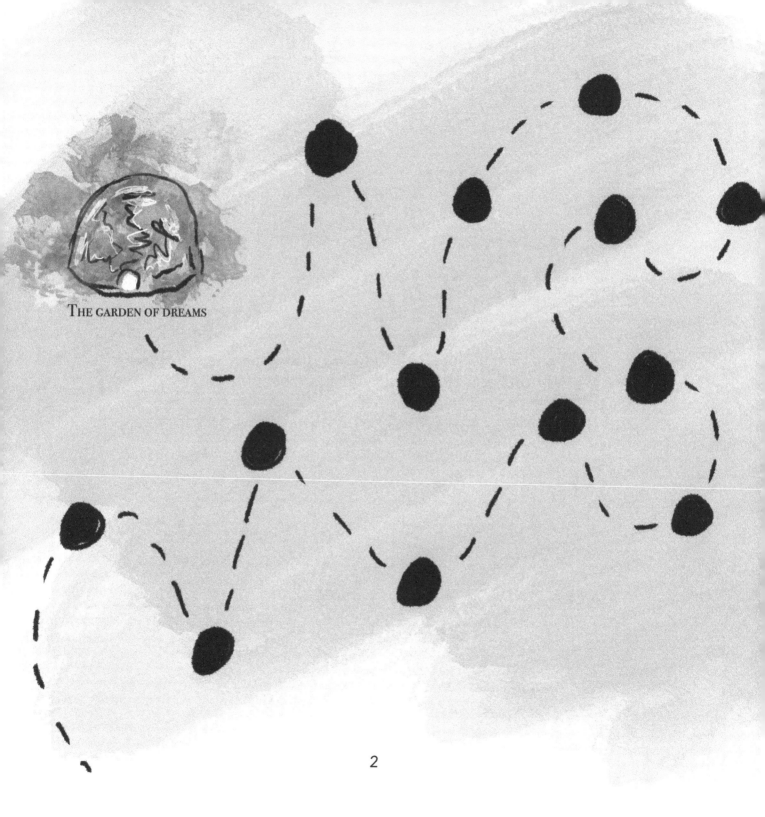

THE GARDEN OF DREAMS

Noah, Max and Tabby loved their new house.

It was a small cottage called Garden's Gate and it had a pretty garden with a big bell in the middle of it.

Gardens Gate

3

One day, the children were playing hide and seek when Max found a secret slide in the attic.

But where did it go?

The children wanted to know so they slid down one after another.

Whee!

The slide came out onto a huge ship that was sailing through the clouds.

"Arr, welcome to The Garden of Dreams," said a pirate.

The children stepped off the ship and onto a cloud, where they listened to the pirate's story.

"My Name is Redbeard and I live here in The Garden of Dreams. It's usually a lovely place but recently it's been getting darker. Let me show you something."

6

Redbeard led the children to the top of a huge hill
and on the other side was a giant dome.

"That's the dream dome," he said.

On one side it was bright with lightning bolts and the other side was as dark as night.

"The darkness is spreading, soon there will be no more light in the dream dome and when that happens, no-one will ever dream again!"

The pirate told them it was his job to find out why.

The children said they would help him.

They sailed through stormy cloud seas
and over huge mountains until they
came to a field of giant daisies.

Above the field was a giant rainbow.

The pirate told them that usually there was
a pot of gold at the end of it.

The children were so excited they ran into the field
of flowers but something stopped them!

A tall woman dressed in white had two giant ants on leads and was running towards the children.

The children screamed and ran away, the pirate followed.

The woman in white shouted at the ants,
"CATCH THEM!"

The children ran until
they reached the end of
the rainbow but instead
of a big pot of gold there
was a big bottle of bright
lightning bolts.

The pirate shouted at the ants,
"STOP!"
And he drew his sword,
cutting their leads.

The woman in white stopped
and the ants turned to face her.
One of them growled at her and
she ran away as fast as she could.

When the woman in white was long gone,
the ants turned to the pirate and children.

"Thank you for saving us from the
Moon Witch, she's evil. She made us
steal the lightning bolts so that her
tower would be the brightest place
all around. We're very sorry,
we were just scared."

The pirate said "We need those back,
otherwise no-one will ever dream again.
Could you help us carry them?"

The ants said "Yes," and soon they were
all back at the dream dome.

The pirate opened one of the bottles and poured the lightning into the dome, the children helped with the other bottles.

The dark side of the dome started to glow brightly and soon the whole thing was bright all over.

"Thank you all for your help," the pirate said and pulled out three golden coins from his pocket, handing them over to the children.

The coins twinkled in their hands.

Somewhere in the distance, a bell started to ring,
getting louder with every ding.

The pirate said, "That's the bell from your garden,
it's very special. When it rings you must find the river
and get on the boat that will take you home.
If you miss the boat, you will be stuck here forever!"

The pirate showed them the river, where a little log boat was waiting.

"One more thing, children: don't ever go down the secret slide after dark." he said.

The children got on the boat and it started to move away.
The pirate waved them goodbye.

The water got faster and faster, rougher and rougher until...

...they were back on the
little stream outside
their house, home safe.

But somewhere in The Garden of Sweets,
the Moon Witch was making plans to do
something terrible...

9 781803 810331